D0060153

Put Beginning Readers on the Right Track with
ALL ABOARD READING™

The All Aboard Reading series is especially for beginning readers. Written by noted authors and illustrated in full color, these are books that children really and truly *want* to read—books to excite their imagination, tickle their funny bone, expand their interests, and support their feelings. With four different reading levels, All Aboard Reading lets you choose which books are most appropriate for your children and their growing abilities.

Picture Readers—for Ages 3 to 6
Picture Readers have super-simple texts, with many nouns appearing as rebus pictures. At the end of each book are 24 flash cards—on one side is the rebus picture; on the other side is the written-out word.

Level 1—for Preschool through First-Grade Children
Level 1 books have very few lines per page, very large type, easy words, lots of repetition, and pictures with visual "cues" to help children figure out the words on the page.

Level 2—for First-Grade to Third-Grade Children
Level 2 books are printed in slightly smaller type than Level 1 books. The stories are more complex, but there is still lots of repetition in the text, and many pictures. The sentences are quite simple and are broken up into short lines to make reading easier.

Level 3—for Second-Grade through Third-Grade Children
Level 3 books have considerably longer texts, harder words, and more complicated sentences.

All Aboard for happy reading!

For my wonderful nieces—
Megan, Sarah, and Anastasia
—P. D.

For my mother and Morgan
—M.M.

Text copyright © 1996 by Patricia Demuth. Illustrations copyright © 1996 by Michael Montgomery. All rights reserved. Published by Grosset & Dunlap, Inc., which is a member of The Putnam & Grosset Group, New York. ALL ABOARD READING is a trademark of The Putnam & Grosset Group. GROSSET & DUNLAP is a trademark of Grosset & Dunlap, Inc. Published simultaneously in Canada. Printed in the U.S.A.

Library of Congress Cataloging-in-Publication Data

Demuth, Patricia.
    Johnny Appleseed / by Patricia Demuth ; illustrated by Michael Montgomery.
        p.   cm. — (All aboard reading. Level 1)
    Summary: Recounts the story of the man who traveled west planting apple seeds to make the country a better place to live.
    1. Appleseed, Johnny, 1774–1845—Juvenile literature.   2. Apple growers—United States—Biography—Juvenile literature.   3. Frontier and pioneer life—Middle West—Juvenile literature.   [1. Appleseed, Johnny, 1774–1845.   2. Apple growers.   3. Frontier and pioneer life.]   I. Montgomery, Michael, 1952-   .   II. Title.   III. Series.
    SB63.C46D45   1996
    634'.11'092—dc20   96-4015
    [B]   CIP
                                                                                                        AC

ISBN 0-448-41131-8 (GB)   D E F G H I J
ISBN 0-448-41130-X (pbk.)   E F G H I J

ALL
ABOARD
READING™

Level 1
Preschool-Grade 1

Johnny Appleseed

By Patricia Demuth

Illustrated by Michael Montgomery

CONTRA COSTA COUNTY LIBRARY

Grosset & Dunlap • New York

WITHDRAWN

3 1901 02755 3553

Who was Johnny Appleseed?

Was he just in stories?

No.

Johnny was a real person.

His name was John Chapman.

He planted apple trees—

lots and lots of them.

So people called him

Johnny Appleseed.

Johnny was young
when our country was young.
Back then many people
were moving West.

There were no towns,
no schools,
not even many houses.
And there were no apple trees.
None at all.

Johnny was going West, too.
He wanted to plant apple trees.
He wanted to make the West
a nicer place to live.
So Johnny got a big, big bag.
He filled it with apple seeds.

Then he set out.

Johnny walked for days
and weeks.

On and on.

Soon his clothes were rags.

His feet were bare.

And what kind of hat
did he wear?

A cooking pot!

That way he didn't
have to carry it.

Snow came.

Did Johnny stop?

No.

He made snowshoes.
Then he walked
some more.

Spring came.

Johnny was out West now.

He stopped by a river.

He dug a hole.

Inside he put an apple seed.

Then he covered it with dirt.

Someday an apple tree
would stand here.
Johnny set out again.
He had lots more
seeds to plant.

Johnny walked by himself.
But he was not alone.

The animals were his friends.

Most people were afraid
of wild animals.
They had guns to shoot them.
But not Johnny.
One day a big, black bear
saw Johnny go by.
It did not hurt Johnny.
Maybe the bear knew
Johnny was a friend.

The Indians were
Johnny's friends, too.

They showed him how to find
good food—
berries and plants and roots.

Where did Johnny sleep?

Under the stars.

Johnny liked to lie on his back
and look up.

The wind blew softly.

Owls hooted.

The stars winked down at him.

Many years passed.
Johnny planted apple trees
everywhere.
People started to call him
Johnny Appleseed.

One day he came back to where
he had planted the first seed.
It was a big tree now.
A girl was swinging in it.

That night Johnny stayed
with the girl's family.
He told stories.
Everybody liked Johnny.
"Stay with us," they said.
"Make a home here."

But Johnny did not stay.

"I have work to do,"

he said.

"I am happy.

The whole world

is my home."

More and more people
came out West.
Johnny planted
more and more trees.
In the spring, the trees bloomed
with white flowers.

In the fall,
there were apples—
red, round, ripe apples.

People made apple pies.

And apple butter for their bread.

And apple cider to drink.
And children had apple trees
to climb.

It was all thanks
to Johnny Appleseed.